Sons and Lovers

Gertrude Morel is poor and unhappily married. Her husband Walter is rough and insensitive, spending much of his free time in the pub. Mrs Morel turns instead to her children, especially her three sons. At first William, the eldest, is her favourite. He gets a job in London and it looks as if he will succeed in life. Tragically, however, he dies suddenly at the age of 23. Mrs Morel now gives all her love and attention to Paul, the second son.

This moving story describes family life in a coalminer's family around the beginning of the twentieth century; and the emotional development of Paul, torn between his passionate love for his mother and his romantic friendships with two young women, Miriam and Clara.

David Herbert Lawrence was born in the mining village of Eastwood, near Nottingham, in 1885, the fourth of five children. *Sons and Lovers*, which appeared in 1913, is perhaps his most famous novel and is based on his own family life. He trained as a school teacher and taught at a school in the south of England from 1908 to 1911.

That year saw the publication of his first novel, *The White Peacock*, the death of his mother and the end of his teaching because of a serious illness. He then went abroad, first to Germany and later to Italy, with Frieda Weekley, the German wife of a professor at Nottingham University. They got married on their return to England in 1914.

Lawrence was now a full-time professional writer, writing not only novels but plays, poems, short stories and travel books. Unhappy in England, he again went to live abroad and he and Frieda lived a mostly wandering life, visiting Italy, Sri Lanka, Australia, New Mexico and Mexico for different periods of time. In Britain he was very much criticised both for the sexual frankness of his writings and for his opposition to the First World War.

Extremely ill with tuberculosis, he died in the south of France at the early age of 44. He is now recognised as one of the most important British writers of the twentieth century.

For a complete list of the titles available in the Penguin Readers series please write to the following address for a catalogue: Penguin ELT Marketing Department, Penguin Books Ltd, 27 Wrights Lane, London W8 5TZ.

Sons and Lovers

D. H. LAWRENCE

Level 5

Retold by J. Y. K. Kerr
Series Editors: Andy Hopkins and Jocelyn Potter

Addison Wesley Longman Limited
Edinburgh Gate, Harlow,
Essex CM20 2JE, England
and Associated Companies throughout the world.

ISBN 0 582 40269 7

First published 1913
This adaptation first published by Penguin Books 1996
This edition first published 1998

Text copyright © J.Y. K. Kerr 1996
Illustrations copyright © Victor Ambrus 1996
All rights reserved

The moral right of the adapter and of the illustrator has been asserted

Typeset by Datix International Limited, Bungay, Suffolk
Set in 11/14pt Lasercomp Bembo
Printed in Spain by Mateu Cromo, S.A. Pinto (Madrid)

Published by Addison Wesley Longman Limited in association with
Penguin Books Ltd., both companies being subsidiaries of Pearson Plc

Dictionary words:

● As you read this book, you will find that some words are in darker black ink than the others on the page. Look them up in your dictionary, if you do not already know them, or try to guess the meaning of the words first, and then look them up later, to check.

CHAPTER ONE

The Early Years

The Morel family lived in the village of Bestwood in a house built by the **mining** company for its employees. Gertrude Morel was thirty-one years old and had been married for eight years. Her husband, Walter, was a coalminer. There were two children: William, a boy of seven, and Annie, who was only five. Mrs Morel was expecting her third baby in two months' time. They could not afford to have this third: she did not want it. Its father spent most of his free time drinking in the pub. She had no respect for him but she was tied to him. She was sick of it, this struggle with poverty and ugliness and dirt.

Gertrude Morel was from a Nottingham family: educated, church-going people. Her father was an unsuccessful engineer. She had her mother's small, well-made figure and her father's clear blue eyes. When she was twenty-three years old, she met, at a Christmas party, a young man of twenty-seven. Walter had shining, black, wavy hair and a black beard. He laughed often and heartily, with a rich, ringing laugh. He was quick in his movements, an excellent dancer. He was so open and pleasant with everybody. Gertrude, who was not pleasure-loving like Walter, had never met anyone like him. His body burned with a soft golden flame, the flame of life, and seemed to her something wonderful.

Walter Morel was equally impressed by Gertrude: her blue eyes, her soft brown curls, her beautiful smile. She spoke in an educated way, she had the manners of a lady. The next Christmas they were married and for three months she was perfectly happy. She admired him for being a miner, risking his life daily. Sometimes when she herself was tired of lovetalk, she tried to open her heart seriously to him. He listened to her respectfully but without understanding. She realised that she could not share her deeper thoughts and ideas with him. Instead, he took pleasure in making and mending, doing little jobs around the house.

Her first big shock was when she found that the bills for their new furniture were not yet paid; and that he did not own their house, as he had told her, but was paying rent – and too high a rent – for it. Then he began to be rather late coming home.

'They're working very late these days, aren't they?' she said to a neighbour.

'No later than they always do,' she answered. 'But they stop to have a drink at the pub and then they get talking. Dinner's stone cold and it's just what they deserve!'

'But Mr Morel doesn't drink.'

The woman looked hard at Mrs Morel, then went on with her work, saying nothing.

Mrs Morel was very ill when the first boy was born. Morel was good to her but she felt very lonely, miles away from her own people. When her husband was with her, it made the loneliness worse. The child was small and weak at first but he quickly grew strong. He was a beautiful baby, with dark golden curls and dark blue eyes, which gradually changed to a clear grey. He came just when her disappointment was at its greatest and her life seemed most empty. She gave all her attention to her child and the father was jealous. While the baby was still small, it often annoyed Morel, and sometimes he hit it. Then Mrs Morel hated her husband for days. Feeling unloved, Morel went out and drank. On his return she greeted him with fierce, stinging remarks about his drinking.

Morel always rose early, about five or six, even on a holiday. On Sunday morning he usually got up and prepared breakfast. The child rose with his father, while the mother lay resting for another hour or so. William was now one year old and his mother was proud of him, he was so pretty. One Sunday morning Mrs Morel lay listening to the two of them talking below. Then she fell asleep. When she came downstairs, there was a big fire burning and breakfast was laid. Morel sat in his armchair, looking rather shamefaced. The child stood between his legs, his head of hair cut short like a sheep; and on a newspaper spread out in front of the fire lay William's golden curls, shining in the firelight. Mrs Morel stood quite still and went very white.

'So what do you think of him?' laughed Morel, a little guiltily.

She came forward, ready to hit him. 'I could kill you, I could!' she said, so angry she could hardly speak. She picked up the child, buried her face in his shoulder and cried painfully. Morel sat looking at the fire in shock. Later she said she had been silly, the boy's hair had to be cut sooner or later. But she remembered this event for the rest of her life. Before, she had wanted to bring her husband closer to her. From now on he was an outsider. This made her life easier to accept. The pity was, she was too much his opposite. In trying to make him better than he was, she destroyed him.

◆

The Morels were poor. Morel was expected to give his wife thirty shillings* a week to pay for everything: rent, food, clothes, insurance, doctors. Sometimes it was a little more, more often less. On Friday night, and Saturday and Sunday,

* There were twenty shillings in a pound and twelve pence in a shilling.

'I could kill you, I could!' Mrs Morel said, so angry she could
hardly speak.

Morel spent freely, mostly on beer. He rarely gave William an extra penny or a pound of apples.

One public holiday he decided to walk to Nottingham with Jerry Purdy, one of his drinking companions. They spent most of the day visiting pubs. Mrs Morel had stayed at home all day, working in the house. In the evening Morel returned, kicking open the garden gate and breaking the lock. He entered the kitchen unsteadily and nearly upset a bowl of boiling liquid which was cooling on the table.

'God help us, coming home in his drunkenness!' cried Mrs Morel.

'Coming home in his what?' shouted her husband, his hat over one eye.

'Say you're *not* drunk!' she insisted.

'Only a nasty old cat like you could have such a thought,' answered Morel.

'You've been drinking all day, so if you're not drunk by eleven o'clock at night—' she replied. 'We know well enough what you do when you go out with your beautiful Jerry. There's money to drink with, if there's money for nothing else.'

'I've not spent two shillings all day,' he said.

'Well, if Jerry's been buying your drinks, tell him to spend his money on his children — they need it! And what about your own children? You can't afford to keep them, can you?'

'What's it got to do with you?' he shouted.

'Got to do with me? Why, a lot! You give me just twenty-five shillings to do everything with, you go off drinking all day, come rolling home at midnight—'

'It's a lie, it's a lie — shut your face, woman!'

The quarrel got fiercer and fiercer. Each forgot everything except their hatred of the other. She was just as angry as he.

'You're a liar!' he shouted, banging on the table with his hand. 'You're a liar! You're a liar!'

All the dislike she felt for him now came pouring out.

'You're nothing but dirt in this house!' she cried.

'Then get out of it – it's mine! It's me who brings the money home, not you. So get out! Get out!'

'And I would,' she cried in tears at her own powerlessness. 'I would have gone long ago, but for those children. Do you think I stay for *you*?'

He came up to her and held her arms tightly. She cried out, struggling to be free. He took her roughly to the outside door and pushed her out of the house, banging the door shut and locking it behind her. Then he sank exhausted into a chair and soon lost consciousness. She stood for a few moments staring helplessly in the August night, her body shaking, remembering the unborn child inside her. The darkness was full of the sweet smell of flowers. There was no noise anywhere. Then a train rushed across the valley miles away. She went to the back door and tried the handle. It was still locked. Through the window she could just see her husband's head on the table and his arms spread out. She knocked on the window more and more loudly but still he did not wake. Fearful for the unborn child, she walked up and down the garden path to keep warm, knocking every now and then on the window, telling herself that in the end he must wake. At last he heard the knocking and woke up.

'Open the door, Walter,' she said coldly.

Realising what he had done, he hurried to unlock the door. As Mrs Morel entered, she saw him disappearing shamefacedly up the stairs. When at last she herself went to bed, Morel was already asleep.

CHAPTER TWO

The Birth of Paul

Before the baby was born, Mrs Morel cleaned the house from top to bottom. When Morel got home one evening, the child had already arrived. The delivery nurse met him in the kitchen.

'Your wife is in a bad way. It's a boy child.'

He hung up his coat and then dropped into his chair.

'Have you got a drink?' he asked. The nurse brought him one, then without a word served him his dinner and went back upstairs. He ate his meal, sat for twenty minutes, made up the fire and then unwillingly went up to the bedroom. His face was still black and sweaty as he stood at the end of the bed.

'Well, how are you then?' he asked.

'I shall be all right,' she answered.

'Hm. It's a boy.'

She turned down the blanket and showed him the baby. He pretended to be pleased but she knew he was not much interested. He wanted to kiss her but he did not dare, so he left the room.

Mrs Morel sat looking at her baby and the baby looked up at her. It had blue eyes like her own, which seemed to bring out her most secret thoughts. She no longer loved her husband. She had not wanted this child and there it lay in her arms and pulled at her heart. A wave of hot love went out of her towards the child. She held it close to her face and breast. It had come into the world unloved. She would love it all the more, now it was here.

♦

During these months Morel got angry at the slightest thing. He seemed exhausted by his work. He complained if the fire was low or his dinner was not to his liking. If the children made a noise, he shouted at them in a way that made their mother's blood boil. They hated him and his bad temper.

'Goodness me, man, there isn't a bit of peace while you're in the house,' said Mrs Morel at last.

'I know that. You're never happy till I'm out of your sight,' he answered, and hurried to escape. He was still not home by eleven o'clock. Finally she heard him coming. He had taken his revenge: he was drunk.

'Is there nothing to eat in the house?' he asked roughly.

'You know what there is,' she said coldly.

He leaned unsteadily on the table and pulled at the table drawer to get a knife to cut bread. The drawer stuck, so he pulled harder. It flew right out and spoons, forks, knives fell all over the floor. The baby woke at the noise.

'What are you doing, you drunken fool?' the mother cried.

In trying to fit the drawer back in, it fell, hurting his leg. In his anger he picked it up and threw it at his wife. One of the corners hit her above the eye. Blood ran into her eye and red drops fell on the baby's blanket.

'Did it hit you?' asked Morel, bending over her unsteadily.

'Go away!'

'Let me look at it, woman.'

She smelled the drink on his breath and weakly pushed him away.

He stood staring at her.

'What has it done to you, dear?' he asked.

'You can see what it's done,' she answered.

Mrs Morel would not let him touch her. She cleaned the

wound herself and went upstairs, telling him to mend the fire and lock the door.

'It was her own fault,' he told himself afterwards. Having hurt her, he hated her.

By the following Wednesday he had no money left. He looked inside his wife's purse when she was in the garden with the baby, and took a sixpence. The next day Mrs Morel found the money missing and was sure he had taken it. When he had had his dinner, she said to him coldly: 'Did you take sixpence from my purse last night?'

Although he denied it, she knew he was lying.

'So you steal sixpence from my purse while I'm bringing the washing in,' she said accusingly.

'I'll make you pay for this,' answered Morel. He got washed and went upstairs with a determined expression on his face. Soon afterwards he came down dressed, with his things tied up in an enormous blue handkerchief.

'You'll see me again when you do,' he said.

'It'll be before I want to,' his wife replied.

At that, he marched out of the house with his parcel.

William and Annie were surprised to find their father gone.

'Where's he going to?' asked William.

'I don't know,' said his mother. 'He's taken his things wrapped up in a handkerchief and he says he's not coming back.'

'What shall we do?' cried the boy in alarm.

'Don't worry, he won't go far.'

'But if he doesn't come back?' said Annie fearfully. She and William sat on the sofa and burst into tears. When Mrs Morel went to fetch coal from the coalhouse at the end of the garden, she felt something hidden behind the door. There in the dark was the big blue parcel. She laughed and went back to the house. William and Annie were crying again because she had left them.

'Silly babies,' she said. 'Go down to the coalhouse and look behind the door and *then* you'll see how far he's gone.'

Off they went to look. No longer worried, they went contentedly to bed.

Mrs Morel sat waiting. She was tired of him, tired to death. He had not even had the courage to take his things further than the bottom of the garden. At about nine o'clock he came in, looking guilty. She said nothing. He took off his coat and sat down to take off his boots.

'You'd better fetch your things from the coalhouse before you take your boots off,' she said quietly.

'You can thank your stars I've come back tonight,' he said trying to impress her. He looked such a fool she was not even angry with him; but her heart was bitter because he had once been the man she loved.

CHAPTER THREE

William Takes the Lead

Some time later Morel became seriously ill. His wife nursed him and, being strong, he soon recovered. He depended on her almost like a child and she was more tolerant of him now because she loved him less. Instead, she turned for love and life to the children and he half accepted this, letting them take his place in her heart. When they sat together at night he was restless, feeling a sort of emptiness. Then he went off to bed and she settled down to enjoy herself alone, working, thinking, living.

The baby Paul hated to be touched by him. Usually a quiet

baby, he went stiff in his father's arms and immediately started to scream. He was a pale, rather silent child, and his face often wore a worried or puzzled expression.

Now another baby was coming, the fruit of this time of peace between the parents. This new baby was again a boy, and they called him Arthur. He was very pretty, with a head of golden curls, and he loved his father from the first. Hearing his father's footsteps, he used to wave his arms and laugh.

At the same time William grew bigger and stronger and more active, while Paul, always rather slight, got thinner and followed his mother around like a shadow.

◆

When William was thirteen, his mother got him a job in the Cooperative Society office. His father wanted him to become a miner like himself.

'He's not going down the mine,' said Mrs Morel, 'and there's an end of it. If your mother put you in the mine at twelve, it's no reason why I should do the same with my boy.'

She was very proud of her son. He was a clever boy with an open nature and eyes of the clearest grey. He went to night-school and trained as a clerk. Then he became a teacher at the night-school. He could run like the wind: when he was twelve, he won first prize in a race. He could jump higher and throw farther than any boy in Bestwood.

William began to get ambitious. He gave all his money to his mother. He went about with the sons of shopkeepers and the schoolteacher. He enjoyed all the social and sporting life that Bestwood offered. He also liked dancing, in spite of his mother. He was a great favourite with the ladies and enjoyed telling Paul about his successes. About this time he began to study. With a friend of his he started to learn French and Latin and other things. He and Fred Simpson studied together till midnight, sometimes till one o'clock. Soon he grew pale and Mrs Morel, alarmed, begged him to take better care of his health.

When William was nineteen, he suddenly left the Co-operative office and got a job in Nottingham. Now he had thirty shillings a week instead of eighteen. His mother and father were proud of him. It seemed that he was going to succeed in life. William stayed at his job in Nottingham for a year. He was studying hard but he still went to all the dances and parties. Then he was offered a position in London at a hundred and twenty pounds a year.

'They want me in Lime Street on Monday week, Mother,' he cried, his eyes shining as he read the letter. Mrs Morel felt everything go silent inside her.

'Didn't I tell you I could do it? Think of me in London! And I can give you twenty pounds a year, Mother. We shall all be rolling in money.'

'We shall, my son,' she answered sadly.

As the day of his departure came closer, she felt increasingly desperate. She loved him so much and now he was going away. She felt that he was going out of her heart, leaving her only pain and sadness.

Before he left – he was just twenty – William burned his file of love-letters from his lady-friends. Then he went off to London to start a new file.

CHAPTER FOUR

Paul's Childhood

Paul's figure was rather small and slight, like his mother's. His fair hair gradually became dark brown. His eyes were grey. He was a pale, quiet child, who seemed old for his years. He was **sensitive** to what other people felt, especially his mother. When she was upset, he understood and could have no peace.

About this time the family moved to another house near the top of a hill, commanding a fine view of the valley below. After dark Paul used to go out to play under the street lamp with the other children of their street. Then when the miners stopped coming home from the mine, he ran fearfully back to the kitchen. The lamp still burned, the fire shone red, Mrs Morel sat alone. Steam rose from the cooking pot, the dinner plate lay waiting on the table. The whole room seemed to be waiting, waiting for the man who was sitting in his coal dirt, dinnerless, a mile away from home across the darkness, drinking himself drunk.

When Morel did come home, everyone in the house kept quiet because he was dangerous. He ate his food roughly and, when he had finished, pushed all the pots away to lay his head and arms on the table. Then he went to sleep, heavy with beer and tiredness and bad temper.

Morel was shut out from family events. No one told him anything. He was an outsider. The only times he entered family life were when he found jobs to do around the house. Sometimes in the evening he mended boots, or the kettle or the metal bottle for cold tea which he took every day to the mine. Then he always wanted helpers and the children enjoyed helping him. He loved telling young Arthur stories about the little horses that the miners used down in the mine. But these happy evenings only took place if Morel had some job to do. Then he always went to bed early. The children felt safe when their father was in bed.

Mrs Morel had given most of her attention to William but when he went to work in Nottingham and was not so much at home, she made a companion of Paul. The two brothers were a little jealous of each other but at the same time they were good friends.

Friday night was **baking** night and market night, because the wages were paid on Fridays. It was the rule that Paul should stay at home and watch the bread in the oven. He loved to be by himself and draw or read. He was very fond of drawing. Mrs Morel enjoyed her marketing. The market place was always full of women shoppers. She usually quarrelled with the cloth-seller, chatted with the fruit man, laughed with the fish man, was coldly polite to the man selling pots. But this time a little dish decorated with blue flowers caught her eye. He told her it cost sevenpence. She put the dish down and walked away. Suddenly the pot man shouted: 'Do you want it for fivepence?'

She was surprised. She bent down and picked up the dish.

'I'll have it,' she said.

Paul was waiting for her. He loved her homecoming. She was always at her best, tired, happy, weighed down with parcels. She dropped her parcels and her string bag on the table.

'Is the bread done?' she asked, going to the oven.

'The last one is baking,' he replied. 'You needn't look. I haven't forgotten it.'

'How much do you think I bought this for?' she said, taking the dish out of its newspaper wrapping.

'One shilling and threepence,' said Paul.

'Five pence!'

The two stood together admiring the dish. She unfolded another piece of newspaper and showed him some little flowering plants.

'Fourpence for these.'

'How cheap!' he cried.

'Yes, but I couldn't afford it this week of all weeks.' Yet she was full of satisfaction.

They were very poor that autumn. William had just gone to London and his mother missed his money. He sent ten shillings once or twice but he had many expenses. He wrote to his mother regularly once a week. He told her all his doings, how he made friends, how he was enjoying London. All day long as she cleaned the house, she thought of him. He was in London: he would do well.

William was coming home at Christmas for five days. There had never been such preparations. Paul and Arthur decorated the kitchen with green leaves. Annie made pretty strings of coloured paper. Mrs Morel baked a special fruit cake, a big rice cake, little cheese cakes. Everything was decorated. A great fire burned. The smell of fresh baking filled the kitchen. William was due at seven o'clock but he was late. The children had gone to the station to meet him. Morel sat in his armchair full of nervous excitement and Mrs Morel quietly went on with her baking. Neither one spoke. They waited and waited.

At last there was the sound of voices and footsteps.

'He's here!' cried Morel, jumping up.

The door burst open and William came in. He dropped his bag and took his mother in his arms. For two seconds, no longer, she held him and kissed him. Then she stood back and, trying to be normal, said: 'But how late you are!'

'Aren't I?' he cried, turning to his father. 'Well, Dad!'

'Well, my boy!' Morel's eyes were wet. 'We thought you were never coming.'

The two men shook hands.

'Everything's just as it was,' said William, looking round. Everybody was still for a second. Then he leaned forward, picked up a newly baked biscuit and put it whole into his mouth.

He had brought them endless presents. Every penny he had, he had spent on them. For his mother there was an umbrella with gold on the handle, which she kept till her dying day. There were pounds of wonderful sweets, quite unknown in Bestwood. Everybody in the family was mad with happiness.

People came in to see William, to see what a difference London had made to him. They all found him 'such a gentleman, such a fine young man, my word!'

When he went away again, the children were in tears, Morel took himself off to bed and Mrs Morel did all her housework mechanically, robbed of all feeling for days.

CHAPTER FIVE

Paul Faces Life

Morel was careless of danger. About a year after William went to London, and just after Paul had left school, before he got work, a great piece of rock fell on Morel's leg when he was working in the mine, and broke it in several places. He had a very bad time in hospital. For a week he was in a serious condition, then he began to mend. Knowing that he was going to recover, the family began to worry less

'Everything's just as it was,' said William, looking round.

and to be happy again. Mrs Morel talked to Paul almost as if she was thinking aloud, and he listened as best he could. In the end she shared almost everything with him. Together, they learned how perfectly peaceful the home could be.

Paul was now fourteen years old and looking for work. His face had lost its boyish roundness and was rather rough-looking but very expressive. He was quite a clever painter for a boy of his age and he knew some French, German and mathematics. He was not strong enough for hard physical work, his mother said. He did not care for making things with his hands but preferred going for country walks, or reading, or painting.

'What do you want to be?' his mother asked. He had no idea.

'Anything.'

'That's no answer,' said Mrs Morel. But it was the only answer he could give.

'Then you must look in the paper for advertisements,' said his mother. He copied out some advertisements and took them to her.

'Yes,' she said, 'you may try.'

He used a letter which William had prepared for him to write to the different companies offering jobs. His handwriting was terrible.

♦

William wrote from London in a kind of fever. He seemed unsettled by the speed of his new life. His mother could feel him losing himself. He wrote of dances and going to the theatre, of boats on the river, of going out with friends. But she knew he sat up afterwards in his cold bedroom, studying Latin and learning all he could about the law, because he wanted to improve himself. He never sent his mother any money now. It was all taken, the little he had, for his own life. Mrs Morel still dreamed of William and what he could do; but in her heart she was worried.

He also wrote a lot now about a girl he had met at a dance, Lily Western. His pet name for her was 'Gypsy'. She was young, beautiful, very well-dressed and much admired by men. His mother congratulated him in her doubtful fashion. She imagined him tied to an expensive wife. 'I'm very likely an old silly,' she told herself, 'expecting the worst.' But the worry remained that William would do the wrong thing.

Soon Paul was asked to go for an interview at Thomas Jordan, Maker of Medical **Appliances**, at 21, Spaniel Row, Nottingham. Mrs Morel was delighted.

'You see,' she cried, her eyes shining, 'you've only written four letters and the third is answered. I always said you were lucky.'

Paul looked at the picture of the wooden leg wearing an **elastic stocking** that appeared on Mr Jordan's notepaper. He had not known that elastic stockings existed.

Mother and son set off one very hot morning in August. Paul felt extremely nervous but he refused to tell his mother and she only partly guessed. They travelled the sixteen miles to Nottingham by train. Mother and son walked down Station Street, feeling the excitement of lovers sharing an adventure. They turned up a narrow street that led to the Castle and found the Thomas Jordan sign. They went through a big doorway into an open space full of boxes and packing stuff, and up two lots of stairs. In front of them was a dirty glass door with the company name on it. Mrs Morel pushed open the door and stood in pleased surprise. They were in a large workshop with thick paper parcels piled everywhere, and clerks with their sleeves rolled up, calmly going about their business.

'Can I see Mr Jordan?' she asked one of the clerks.

'I'll fetch him,' answered the young man and went to a glass office at the far end of the room. A red-faced old man with white hair came towards them. He had short legs and was rather fat. They followed him to his office and were told to sit down.

'Did you write this letter?' he asked Paul, holding it up.

'Yes,' he answered.

'Where did you learn to write?'

Paul simply looked at him, too ashamed and nervous to speak.

'And you say you know French?' asked the little man sharply.

'A friend gave him lessons,' said Mrs Morel quickly.

Mr Jordan hesitated, then pulled a sheet of paper from his pocket and passed it to Paul.

'Read that,' he said.

It was a letter in French in strange, spidery, foreign hand-writing which was very difficult to read. Paul struggled with the words: 'Please send me . . . two pairs . . . of grey cotton stockings . . . without fingers . . .'

'Without toes!' the factory owner corrected him. 'Stockings don't have fingers.'

Paul hated the little man for making him look stupid.

'When can he start?' Mr Jordan asked his mother.

It was agreed that Paul would be employed as a junior clerk at eight shillings a week. As he followed his mother down the stairs on their way out, she looked at him with her blue eyes full of delighted love.

On the Monday morning Paul got up at six, to be ready for work. He had bought his season ticket for the train at a cost of one pound eleven shillings, and his mother had packed his dinner in a small basket. She stood in the road, watching him as he crossed the fields to the station. Now she had two sons in the world: one in London and one in Nottingham. They came from her and their work would also be hers. All morning she thought of Paul.

At the factory Paul was told to work with Mr Pappleworth, an amusing man who was about thirty-six years old. Pappleworth showed him what to do. They had to read the letters ordering different appliances, note down each order in a big book, write out the exact details on a yellow order paper and take the order to one of the departments to be made. Most of the orders were for elastic stockings or bandages. Later, he was introduced to Polly and the girls downstairs, and then Fanny and the girls upstairs. At one o'clock Paul ate his dinner and then he went out into the brightness and freedom of the streets until two. In the afternoon there was not very much to do. At five o'clock all the men went downstairs and had tea. After tea the gas lights were lit. Paul had done his paperwork and now he had to pack up the finished goods in parcels, writing the address and putting the right stamps on each one. At last he was free to grab his dinner basket and run to the station in time for the 8.20 train. His day in the factory was exactly twelve hours long.

He did not get home that evening till twenty past nine. He was pale and tired but his mother saw that he was rather pleased. He told her everything, all he had seen, all he thought, every detail of the experience.

So the time passed happily enough. The factory was a friendly place. Nobody was rushed or driven too hard and every Friday night he put his eight shillings proudly on the kitchen table. Then he told his mother the happenings of the day. It was almost as if it was her own life.

CHAPTER SIX

Death in the Family

Arthur Morel was growing up. He was quick and careless, rather like his father. He hated study and hard work. He was the flower of the family, a well-made boy with fair hair, fresh colouring and wonderful dark blue eyes. He had a quick temper and thought only of himself. He loved his mother but she got tired of him sometimes. He had loved his father, and Morel still thought the world of him but now Arthur had come to hate him. His father's manners in the home got worse and worse. When they got too much for him, Arthur used to jump up and leave the house. He got so bad-tempered that, when he won a place at the Grammar School in Nottingham, his mother sent him to live with one of her sisters, and so he only came home at weekends.

Annie was a junior teacher at Bestwood School, earning about four shillings a week. But soon she would get fifteen shillings, because she had passed her examination. That would make the financial situation in the home a bit easier.

William was now **engaged** to his girl and had bought her an engagement ring. He wanted to bring her home at Christmas. This time William arrived with the lady but with no presents. Mrs Morel had prepared supper. He kissed his mother hurriedly and then stood back to introduce a tall, handsome, young woman, very fashionably dressed.

'Here's Gyp!'

Miss Western held out her hand and showed her teeth in a small smile.

'Oh, how do you do, Mrs Morel,' she said.

'I'm afraid you will be hungry,' said Mrs Morel.

'Oh no, we had dinner in the train.' She looked round the kitchen. It seemed small and curious to her, with the green leaves decorating the pictures and the rough little table. Annie showed her up to the front bedroom where the parents usually slept, then returned to fetch hot water. After half an hour Miss Western came down wearing another fine dress. Morel pressed her to take his armchair beside the fire. The three children sat round in silent admiration. At ten o'clock she shook hands all round and departed to bed, led by William. In five minutes he was downstairs again but he talked very little until he was alone with his mother. His heart was rather sore, he did not know why.

'Well, mother, do you like her?'

'Yes,' came the cautious reply.

'She's not like you, mother. She's not serious, and she can't think. Her mother died when she was a child. She's had no love. I know she seems shallow. You have to forgive her a lot of things.'

'You mustn't judge too quickly,' said Mrs Morel.

But William remained uncomfortable within himself.

Lily continued to play the fine lady. She sat and let Annie or Paul act as her servants. And yet she was not so fine. For a year now, she had been some sort of secretary or clerk in a London office.

At Easter William came home alone; and he discussed Lily endlessly with his mother.

'You know, mother, when I'm away from her, I don't care for her a bit. But then when I'm with her in the evenings, I'm awfully fond of her.'

'It's a strange sort of love to marry on,' said Mrs Morel, 'if she holds you no more than that.'

◆

Paul's wages had been increased at Christmas to ten shillings a week. He was quite happy at Jordan's but his health suffered from the long hours and the bad air. His mother wanted to help. His half-day holiday was on Monday afternoon. At breakfast one Monday in May, Mrs Morel told Paul that her friend Mrs Leivers had invited them to visit her at their new farm. It was agreed that mother and son would go that afternoon: a four mile walk. They set off in style: Mrs Morel with the umbrella William had given her, because of the sun.

After walking for a long time, they finally came to a group of low, red farm buildings. There were apple trees and a pool with ducks. Some cows stood under the trees. As they entered the garden, a girl appeared in the doorway of the house. She was about fourteen, with short, dark curls and dark eyes. She disappeared. In a minute another figure appeared, a small woman, also with great dark brown eyes.

'Oh!' she said smiling. 'You've come then. I *am* glad to see you.' She introduced the girl with the dark curls as her daughter Miriam. The four of them had tea together. Then they went out for a walk in the wood. Both mother and son were thrilled by the beauty of the place. When they got back to the house, they found Mr Leivers and Edgar, the eldest son, in the kitchen. Edgar was about eighteen. Then the two younger boys came in from school. The boys all went outside and played games. Miriam watched but did not join in. She was very shy.

Finally it was time for the Morels to go home. Mr and Mrs Leivers walked over the fields with them for part of the way. Paul was carrying a great bunch of flowers Mrs Leivers had given them. The hills were golden with evening: everywhere was perfectly still. Mrs Morel and Paul went on alone together.

'Wasn't it lovely, mother?' he said quietly. He felt almost painfully happy.

◆

William came home again with his young lady for a week's holiday. There was a feeling of sadness and tenderness in the house while they were there. But William often got annoyed. For an eight days' stay, Lily had brought five dresses and six blouses.

'Oh, could you please wash these two blouses and these other things?' she said to Annie.

And Annie stayed washing while William and Lily went out. This made Mrs Morel extremely angry. William read a lot and had a quick, active mind; but Lily found reading difficult. She understood nothing but love-making and social chat. She could not give him real companionship.

'She wants to get married,' he told his mother, 'and I think we might get married next year.'

'A fine mess of a marriage it would be,' answered his mother. 'I should consider it again, my boy. Nothing is as bad as a failed marriage. Mine was bad enough, God knows.'

'I couldn't give her up now,' said William.

'Well, remember there are worse wrongs than breaking off an engagement.'

Before he left, William remarked to his mother: 'Gyp's very fond of me now. But if I die, she'll forget me in three months.'

Mrs Morel was afraid. Her heart beat wildly, hearing the bitterness in her son's words.

He came home again in October, this time also alone. He was thinner than ever. He was doing extra work, trying to make some money to get married with. On the Sunday morning, as he was putting his collar on, he showed his mother an ugly red mark under his chin.

Three days after he left, a telegram came from London, saying that he was ill. Mrs Morel read the telegram, borrowed some money, put on her best clothes and set off. It was six o'clock when she arrived at William's address.

'How is he?' she asked the house-owner.

'No better,' she told her. William lay on the bed, his eyes red, his face discoloured. There was no fire in the room. No one had been with him. He looked at her but did not see her: he was quite unconscious.

'How long has he been like this?' asked Mrs Morel.

'He got home at six o'clock on Monday morning and slept all day. The next morning he asked for you, so I sent you a telegram and fetched the doctor.'

The doctor came again. It was a chest infection, he said, and 'erysipelas', a rare skin disease. He hoped it would not get to the brain.

Mrs Morel settled down to nurse. That night she prayed for William, prayed that at least he would recognise her but his condition got rapidly worse. At two o'clock in the morning he died. Mrs Morel sat perfectly still for an hour in William's bedroom. When day came, she sent a telegram.

'William died last night. Let father come. Bring money.'

Morel had only once before been in London. Nervously he set off to help his wife. They returned to Bestwood on Saturday night, having walked from the station. In the house Mrs Morel was white and silent. All she said was: 'The **coffin** will be here tonight, Walter. You'd better arrange for some help.' Then, turning to the children: 'We're bringing him home.'

In the front room Morel arranged six chairs opposite each other for the coffin to stand on. At ten o'clock there was the

*Six miners in their shirtsleeves came up the narrow garden path,
holding the coffin high.*

noise of wheels. Arthur held one **candle**, Annie another. Outside in the darkness Paul could see horses, a lamp and a few pale faces. Six miners in their shirtsleeves came up the narrow garden path, holding the coffin high.

'Steady, steady!' cried Morel, as if in pain. The six men struggled into the room with the great wooden box. Paul saw drops of sweat fall from his father's face onto the wooden top.

At last the family was alone in the room with the great coffin. The mother was stroking the shining wood.

'Oh my son, my son!' she cried softly. 'Oh my son, my son!'

They buried him on the hillside that looks over towards Bestwood. It was sunny. They laid a bunch of white flowers on the warm earth.

William had been right about Lily. She wrote to Mrs Morel at Christmas: 'I was at a party last night. Some charming people were there. I didn't miss a single dance . . .' After that Mrs Morel never heard from her again.

Then, on 23 December, Paul came home and gave his Christmas money to his mother with shaking hands.

'I feel bad, mother.'

She undressed him and put him to bed. He had a serious chest infection, the doctor said. Paul was very ill. His mother lay in bed with him at night. They could not afford a nurse. He grew worse and the crisis approached. Realising how much his mother was suffering, Paul used all his willpower to hold on to life and finally he began to recover. He was in bed for seven weeks and when he got up, he was weak and pale. Mrs Morel's life now fixed itself on Paul.

CHAPTER SEVEN

Boy and Girl Love

Paul went to Willey Farm many times during the autumn. He made friends with the two younger Leiver boys. Edgar kept his distance at first and Miriam also did not let him approach her. She was deeply romantic by nature. Literature was important to her, and religion. She did not care much about being beautiful and in general she did not think highly of the male sex. But she saw in Paul a new type of male, quick and light, one who could be gentle and sad, who knew a lot and who had had a death in the family.

Gradually he began to spend more time with Miriam. They had a common feeling for things in nature: flowers, trees and birds. She and her mother admired his paintings and encouraged him. One dull afternoon when the others were out, the girl said to him, hesitating:

'Have you seen the **swing**?'

'No,' he answered. 'Where?'

'Come,' she said. 'I'll show you.'

In the cowhouse a great thick rope with a seat on the end hung from the roof. Paul sat down, eager to try it, then immediately rose.

'Come on then and have first go,' he said to her.

'No, I won't go first,' she answered. 'You go!'

'All right,' he said, sitting down again. 'Watch this!'

In a moment he was flying through the air, every bit of him swinging, diving like a bird in the pleasure of movement. He looked down at her. Her red woollen hat hung over her dark curls and her beautiful warm face was lifted towards him. He gradually swung more slowly and jumped off.

'This swing's a real winner!' he cried delightedly.

Miriam was amused that he took the swing so seriously.

'Don't you want to try it?' asked Paul.

'Well – not much. I'll have just a little one.'

He held the seat steady for her, then started her moving.

'Keep your feet up or you'll hit the wall.'

She felt him catch her and push her again and was afraid. Again came his push, at just the right moment.

'Ha,' she laughed in fear. 'No higher!'

'But you're not a *bit* high!' he complained.

'But no higher!'

He heard the fear in her voice and stopped pushing. She felt sure he was going to push her again but no: he left her alone. She swung more slowly and got down. Paul took her place and away he went. For a time he was nothing but a body swinging in space, there was no part of him that did not swing. She could never lose herself like that.

Later on they talked. She was very dissatisfied with her life.

'Just because I'm a girl, why must I stay at home? Why am I not allowed to do anything? What chance do I have?'

'Chance of what?'

'Of knowing anything – of learning – of doing anything. It's not fair, just because I'm a woman.'

'But it's as good to be a woman as a man,' said Paul.

'Ha! – is it? Men have everything.'

'But what do you want?' he asked.

'I want to learn. Why must I know nothing?'

'You mean mathematics and French?'

'Yes, why can't I learn mathematics?' she cried, her eyes widening.

Next time he went up to the farm, he found Miriam cleaning the kitchen.

'Ready to do some mathematics?' he asked, taking a little book from his pocket.

'But–' He could see she was doubtful.

'You said you wanted to,' he insisted.

'Yes, but tonight I wasn't expecting it.'

However, they made a start.

Paul taught Miriam regularly. She had always studied the work from the week before but things came slowly to her. He got angry with her, felt ashamed, continued the lesson, got angry again. She listened in silence. She rarely protested.

'You don't give me time to learn it.'

She was right. It was strange that no one else made him so angry. When he saw her suffering, again he felt pity.

His painting was improving. Mr Jordan had given him Wednesday afternoon off to go to the art school. He loved to sit at home, alone with his mother at night, working and working; but when a drawing was finished, he always wanted to take it to Miriam.

The Bestwood library was open on Thursday evenings. Paul and Miriam were in the habit of meeting there when they changed their library books. Afterwards Paul often went part of the way home with her. Always when he went with Miriam and it got rather late, he knew his mother was worrying and getting angry with him. She did not like Miriam. She felt that the girl was leading Paul away from her. 'She will never let him become a man, she never will,' she thought. So when he was away with Miriam, Mrs Morel got more and more annoyed.

'What are you so displeased about?' he asked. 'Is it because you don't like her?'

'I don't say I don't like her. But I don't agree with young boys and girls staying out late, and never did.'

He kissed her and went slowly to bed. He had forgotten

Miriam. He saw only that his mother was somehow hurt.

Sometimes as they were walking together, Miriam put her arm shyly into his. But he always disliked it and she knew this. He himself did not know what was the matter. He was so young and their **relationship** was so unphysical, he did not know that he really wanted to press her to his breast to reduce the ache there. He was too ashamed to recognise the fact that he might want her as a man wants a woman. Neither of them could face such an idea. And the 'purity' of their feelings prevented even their first love kiss. It was as if she could scarcely accept the shock of physical love, while he was too shy and sensitive to give it.

CHAPTER EIGHT

The Battle of Love

Out of kindness to his mother, Paul did not go much to Willey Farm for a while. He sent two pictures to the autumn **exhibition** of students' work at the Castle Museum and both of them won first prizes. He was most excited and his mother was enormously pleased. William had won sports prizes, which she still kept; she did not forgive his death. Arthur, now in the army, was handsome, warm and generous. He would probably do well in the end. But Paul was going to do something important in life. She believed in him more firmly because he himself did not seem to realise his own capabilities. Life for her was rich with promise. Her struggle had not been for nothing.

Several times during the exhibition Mrs Morel went to the Castle Museum, unknown to Paul. She wandered round the long room, looking at the other pictures. Some made her jealous, they were so good. Then suddenly she had a shock that made her heart beat. There hung Paul's picture!

Name – Paul Morel – First Prize.

She felt a proud woman. When she passed well-dressed ladies going home through the park, she thought to herself: 'Yes, you look very fine but I wonder if *your* son has two first prizes in the exhibition.'

One day Paul met Miriam in the street in Nottingham. He had not expected to meet her in town. She was walking with a rather impressive young woman, fair-haired, with a discontented expression, who held herself boldly upright. It was strange how small Miriam looked beside this woman with the handsome shoulders. Miriam watched Paul closely: his eyes were on the stranger, not on her. She explained that she had driven in to market with her father.

'I've told you about Mrs Dawes,' she said nervously.

'Clara, do you know Paul?'

'I think I've seen him before,' replied Mrs Dawes, showing little interest as she shook hands. She had proud, grey eyes, a skin like white honey and a full mouth with a slightly lifted top lip. Her clothes were simple and rather dull. Clearly she was poor and, unlike Miriam, did not have much taste.

'Where have you seen me?' asked Paul.

'Walking with Louie Travers,' she replied. Louie was one of the girls in the factory.

'How do you know her?' he asked. She did not answer. The two women moved on towards the Castle.

Paul remembered that Clara was the daughter of an old friend of Mrs Leivers. She had once held one of the better jobs at Jordan's and her husband, Baxter Dawes, still worked there, making metal parts. But Mrs Dawes was separated from her husband and had taken up the cause of women. People said she was clever.

He knew Baxter Dawes from work, a big, well-built man of thirty-one or two. He had the same white skin as his wife and a golden moustache; but his eyes moved continually this way and that. He seemed to have little self-respect; usually he was rude and insulting. He and Paul met often enough in the factory and disliked each other. Clara Dawes had no children. She now lived with her mother.

The next time Miriam saw him, she asked: 'What did you think of Clara Dawes?'

'She has a good figure,' answered Paul, 'but she doesn't look very friendly. Is she unpleasant as a person?'

'I don't think so. I think she's discontented – still married to a man like Baxter. What other things did you like about her?'

'Oh, I don't know. Her **passionate** mouth, the shape of her throat, her skin. There's something fierce about her. I think I'd like to do a painting of her.'

Miriam seemed strangely lost in thought.

'You don't really like her, do you?' he asked her.

'Oh yes, I do,' she said.

'Perhaps you like her because she's so much against men.'

Paul was now twenty-one. Mr Jordan had put him in charge of the department where he worked, and had increased his wages to thirty shillings a week. At the Art School he was studying design. He was also helping Miriam to learn French. On Friday evenings, when his father went to the pub and his mother to the market, Paul was left at home to watch the baking of the bread. Annie, who was now engaged to be married to Leonard, her young man, was also out visiting. At a quarter past seven there was a low knock and Miriam came in. He showed her his latest artwork and corrected the French she had written for him. This week she had done well. He loved to talk about his work with Miriam. All his passion went into these conversations. Somehow she lit up his imagination.

'Aren't you forgetting the bread?' Miriam said suddenly.

Paul rushed to open the oven door. Out came bluish smoke. One loaf was hard as a brick, another was burned black along one side. Paul tried to scratch off the burnt part, then wrapped it in a wet towel and left it in the back kitchen. They went back to their French until it was time for Miriam to go home. Paul turned down the gas and they set off.

He did not get home again until a quarter to eleven. His mother was in her chair, reading the local newspaper. Annie was sitting in front of the fire, looking gloomy. The burnt loaf, unwrapped, stood on the table. Paul felt very uncomfortable. For some minutes he sat pretending to read. Then: 'I forgot that bread, mother.' There was no answer from either woman.

'You don't know how ill our mother is,' said Annie after a pause.

'Why is she so ill?' asked Paul sharply.

'She could hardly get home. I found her white as anything, sitting here,' said Annie in a tearful voice.

'I had so many parcels,' said Mrs Morel, 'the meat and the vegetables and a pair of curtains.'

'Let Annie fetch the meat,' said Paul.

'But how was I to know? You were off with Miriam instead of being here when Mother came.'

'And what's the matter with you?' Paul asked his mother.

'I suppose it's my heart,' she replied. She certainly looked bluish round the mouth.

'And have you felt it before?'

'Yes, often enough.'

'Then why haven't you told me, and why haven't you seen a doctor?'

'You'd never notice anything,' said Annie. 'You're too eager to be off with Miriam.'

'So that was why the bread was spoiled,' said Mrs Morel bitterly.

'No, it was not!' he replied angrily.

'I bought you a nice piece of cheese,' said his mother. He was too angry to go and look for it.

'I don't want anything,' he said.

'If I want you to go out on a Friday night, you say you're too tired,' she complained, 'but you're never too tired to go if *she* comes for you.'

'I can't let her go back alone.'

'Can't you? Then why does she come? Because you want her.'

'I do like to talk to her but I don't *love* her,' Paul explained. 'We talk about painting and books. You know you don't care whether a picture is decorative or not.'

'How do you know I don't care?'

'Oh, you're old, mother, and we're young.'

He only meant that the interests of her age group were not the interests of his; but the moment he had spoken, he realised that he had said the wrong thing. It was too painful. He realised that he was life to her. And after all she was the chief thing to him, the only all-important thing.

'No, mother, I really don't love her. I talk to her but I want to come home to you.'

As he bent to kiss his mother, she threw her arms round his neck and cried in a desperate voice quite unlike her own: 'It's too much. I could let another woman but not her. And I've never − you know, Paul − I've never had a husband, not really−'

Immediately he hated Miriam bitterly. His mother kissed him, a kiss of passionate love. Without knowing, he gently stroked her face. At that moment Morel came in, walking unsteadily, his hat over one eye. He paused in the doorway.

'Making more trouble?' he said with an ugly look. Mrs Morel's feelings turned to sudden hatred of her drunken husband.

'At least I'm not drunk,' she said.

Morel disappeared and returned with a piece of cheese in his hand. It was what Mrs Morel had bought for Paul.

'And I didn't buy that for you. If you give me only twenty-five shillings, don't expect me to buy you cheese, when you're already full up with beer!'

'What!' shouted Morel, 'what – not for me?' He looked at the cheese in his hand and suddenly threw it into the fire. Paul jumped to his feet.

'Waste your own food!' he cried.

'What – what!' shouted Morel, taking up a threatening position. 'I'll show you, you cheeky young fool!'

'All right,' said Paul hotly. 'Show me!'

At that moment he wanted to hit his father violently.

'There!' cried Morel, delivering a great blow just past his son's face. Even so close, he did not dare to touch the younger man.

'Right!' said Paul and was preparing to hit his father on the mouth. He ached to land the blow; but he heard a frightened sound behind him. His mother was pale as death, and dark around the lips. Morel was dancing up to deliver another blow.

'Father,' said Paul urgently.

Morel shook and stood still.

'Mother!' cried the boy. 'Mother!'

She began to struggle with herself. She could not move. Gradually she got more control. Paul laid her down on the sofa and ran to fetch her something to drink. The tears were streaming down his face.

'What's the matter with her?' said Morel sitting on the opposite side of the room.

'She's **fainted**!' replied Paul.

Morel took his boots off and went unsteadily to his bed.

Paul knelt there, stroking his mother's hand.

'It's nothing, my boy,' she whispered.

Paul made up the fire, straightened the room, laid the things for breakfast and brought his mother's candle. He followed her up the stairs and kissed her once more.

'Goodnight, Mother.'

'Goodnight!' she said.

In the days that followed, everyone tried to forget what had taken place.

CHAPTER NINE

The Defeat of Miriam

The Easter holiday began happily. Paul rode his bicycle up to Willey Farm. But he was in a hard, critical mood when he went out walking round the farm with Miriam. Paul kept on finding fault with her. They stopped to rest on a bed of dry grass.

'Why are you sad?' she asked gently.

'I'm not sad, why should I be?' he answered. 'I'm only normal.'

She wondered why he always called himself normal when he was unpleasant.

'But what's the matter?' she insisted.

'Nothing.'

He picked up a stick and dug the earth with it in a fever of bad temper. Gently but firmly, she put her hand on his.

'Don't!' she said. 'Put it away.'

He threw the stick into the grass and **leaned** back.

'What is it?' she asked again softly.

He lay quite still with only his eyes alive, and those full of unhappiness.

'You know,' he said finally, his voice rather tired, 'you know, we'd better break off.'

'Why?' she asked. 'What has happened?'

'Nothing has happened. I can only give friendship, I'm not capable of anything more. It's not equal, our relationship. Let's end it.'

He meant that she loved him more than he loved her. She pitied him in his suffering. He felt so ashamed.

'But I don't understand,' she said.

'I know,' he cried, 'you never will. You'll never believe I can't – can't physically, any more than I can fly–'

'Can't what?' she whispered.

'Love you.'

'What have they been saying at home?' she asked.

'It's not that,' he answered.

But she knew it was. They did not talk much more that evening. Instead Paul and Edgar went off on their bicycles.

He had come back to his mother. Hers was the strongest tie in his life. Even Miriam seemed unreal when he thought about her. And in the same way his mother depended on him. Paul was going to change the face of the Earth in some way that really mattered. And yet for Paul it was not enough. His new young life, so strong and commanding, was driving him on toward something else. It made him mad with restlessness.

◆

Miriam had not stopped hoping to win Paul back. He still visited the Leivers but spent most of his time with Edgar.

In May, she asked Paul to come to the farm and meet Mrs Dawes. He was rather excited at the idea of seeing Clara again.

Mrs Dawes came for the day. Her heavy, fair hair was twisted on top of her head. She wore a white blouse and a dark blue skirt. Paul did not come till the afternoon. As he got off his bicycle, Miriam saw him look round eagerly at the house.

'Hasn't Clara come yet?' he asked.

'Yes,' replied Miriam in her musical voice. 'She came this morning. She's reading.'

'And is she any pleasanter?' he asked again.

'You know I always think she's quite pleasant.'

Clara sat inside, reading. Paul saw the back of her white neck with the fine hair lifted up from it. She rose, looking at him without interest. When she shook hands, she seemed to keep him at a distance and yet offer him something. He noticed the roundness of her breasts inside her blouse and the fine curve of her shoulders.

'You've chosen a fine day,' he said.

'It seems so,' she answered.

The conversation continued for a little. Clara did not seem to find Paul's comments at all clever.

'Well, I think I'll go and see Edgar,' he said, and left them.

After tea Mrs Leivers said to Clara: 'And you find life happier now?'

'Much happier.'

'And are you satisfied?'

'If I can remain free and independent, yes.'

'And you don't miss anything in your life?' asked Mrs Leivers gently.

'I've put all that behind me.'

Paul had been listening to this conversation.

'You'll find you're always falling over the things you've put behind you,' he said, and left to find Edgar again. He felt he had been clever and was proud of himself. He whistled as he went.

A little later Miriam came to ask if he would go with her and Clara for a walk. Clara walked in front by herself for part of the way, her head bent. Paul was curious about her. He forgot Miriam, who was walking beside him, talking to him. She looked at him, finding he did not answer her. His eyes were fixed in front on Clara.

'Do you still think she is unpleasant?' she asked.

'Something's the matter with her,' he said.

'Yes,' said Miriam.

They came to a field hidden by trees round the edges. In the smooth grass, beautiful, bright yellow spring flowers were growing. Paul and Miriam started picking them. Clara wandered about looking depressed. Then she knelt down, bending forward to smell the flowers. Her neck looked such a beautiful thing, her breasts swung slightly in her blouse. The curve of her back was beautiful and strong. Suddenly, without realising, Paul was dropping a handful of flowers over her hair and neck. She looked up at him with fear in her grey eyes, wondering what he was doing. Suddenly, standing there above her, he felt uncomfortable. Clara laughed strangely and rose, picking the flowers from her hair. One flower remained caught in her hair. Paul saw but did not tell her. He collected the flowers he had dropped. Unexpectedly, she gave him a grateful smile.

Going down the path, they were all silent. As the evening deepened, they could see the mining village across the valley, little lights on a dark hill touching the sky.

'It's been nice, hasn't it?' said Paul.

Miriam agreed. Clara was silent. He could tell by the way she moved, pretending not to care, that she suffered.

41

Suddenly, without realising, Paul was dropping a handful of flowers over Clara's hair and neck.

At home he told his mother about Clara: that she was poor, that she lived with her mother, that she was thirty years old.

'And what's so charming about her, my boy?' asked his mother.

'I don't know that she's charming, mother, but she's nice. She seems straight, you know, not a bit deep.'

Mrs Morel was not against the idea of Clara.

♦

Annie and Leonard were getting married. She had saved eleven pounds and Leonard twenty-three, so the wedding took place almost immediately. Arthur came home and looked sensational in his army uniform. Annie looked nice in a grey dress she could also use for Sundays. Morel was cool to Leonard. Annie cried her eyes out in the kitchen on leaving her mother. Mrs Morel cried a little, then stroked her and said:

'Don't cry, child, he'll be good to you.'

Afterwards Paul and Mrs Morel were left alone.

'You're not sorry she's married, mother, are you?'

'No, but it seems strange, now she's gone from me. When I think of my own wedding day, I can only hope that her life will be different.

'I'll never marry while I've got you – I won't.'

He kissed her and went to bed.

Mrs Morel sat thinking, about her daughter, about Paul, about Arthur. She was upset at losing Annie. But Paul needed her and Arthur needed her too.

♦

Paul felt life changing around him. Annie was married, Arthur was living his own life of pleasure. For both of them

43

life lay outside their mother's house. They only came home for holidays and rest. Paul dreamed of following them. Yet home for him was beside his mother. He grew more and more restless. Miriam did not satisfy him. His old wish to be with her grew weaker. Sometimes he met Clara in Nottingham, sometimes he saw her at Willey Farm; but between Paul and Clara and Miriam there was always a kind of struggle.

For Miriam's twenty-first birthday Paul wrote her a long, rather philosophical letter, which more or less brought their relationship to an end. He was now twenty-three years old and his sexual need was growing strong. Often when he talked to Clara Dawes, he was conscious of his blood flowing quicker, of something alive in him, of a new self, a new consciousness. He knew that sooner or later his need would have to be satisfied.

CHAPTER TEN

Clara

When he was twenty-three, Paul sent in a painting to the winter exhibition at the Castle Museum. One morning the postman came when Mrs Morel was doing the washing. Suddenly Paul heard a wild noise from his mother. Rushing into the kitchen, he found her screaming and waving a letter, as if she had gone mad. The postman too came running back, afraid something bad had happened.

'His picture's got first prize, Fred,' she cried, 'and it's been sold for twenty pounds!'

'That looks like meaning something!' said the young postman.

44

'Didn't I say we would do it?' she said, pretending she was not crying.

Morel was greatly impressed. 'Twenty pounds for a bit of a painting that took him just an hour or two,' he said amazed. 'Yes, and that other boy would have done as much if they hadn't killed him,' he added quietly. The thought of William went through Mrs Morel like a sharp knife.

◆

Arthur left the army and immediately got married to Beatrice, whom he had known for years. The baby was born six months after the wedding. With the help of Beatrice's mother, Mrs Morel found furniture for a little two-room house. He was caught now. For a while he refused to settle down and got annoyed with his young wife, who loved him. He nearly went mad when the baby cried or gave trouble. He complained for hours to his mother, who only said: 'Well, my son, you did it yourself, now you must make the best of it.' And then the stronger side of his character appeared. He accepted his responsibilities, recognised that he belonged to his wife and child and made a good job of it.

◆

The months passed slowly. One day a friend of Clara's in Bestwood asked Paul to take a message to Mrs Dawes. In the evening after work he went to the house where she lived with her mother. The street was poor and the paint on the front door was old. A large, fat woman of about sixty answered his knock. This was Mrs Radford, Clara's mother. In a moment Clara appeared. Her face went red: she seemed embarrassed that he had discovered her at home like this. She invited him into the kitchen, where the two women spent all their time making **lace**. The room was full of the white snowy stuff. Clara gave him a chair, brought him a beer and went on with her work. Her arm moved mechanically as she used the machine, her head was bent over the lace. Her life seemed so narrow, so limited, Paul thought. Her grey eyes at last met his. He recognised that she was deeply unhappy, a kind of prisoner. He felt shaken. It was not what he had expected. She had seemed so high and proud. He left in a kind of dream.

The girl in charge of the stocking department at Jordan's was leaving to get married. He told Clara about the vacant position. So Clara came back to Jordan's. Now they were fellow-workers and saw each other several times a day. When Paul was painting in the afternoon, she often came and stood near him, keeping perfectly still. Although she stood a yard away, he felt as if she was pressed against him and he was full of her warmth. Then he could paint no more. He threw down the brushes and began to talk.

On Paul's birthday he met Clara by chance in the dinner hour. They decided to go together up to the Castle. At the top they leaned over the wall. Away at the foot of the rock, tiny trees stood in their own pools of shadow, and tiny people went rushing about with amusing self-importance. She disliked towns, Clara told him. 'When things are natural, they're beautiful.'

'And what isn't natural?' asked Paul.

'Everything man has made,' she answered, 'including man himself.'

'But his women made him,' he remarked. 'Wasn't Baxter Dawes natural?'

She changed colour and looked away from him.

'We will not discuss it,' she said.

Later that afternoon the postman brought Paul a small packet. It was a book of poems with a note inside. 'Please allow me to send you this. I am sympathetic to your problems and wish you well. C.D.'

Paul felt deeply moved, and warm towards her. After this they often went out together in the dinner hour. Paul asked her about Dawes.

'How old were you when you married?'

'Twenty-two.'

'That was eight years ago?'

'Yes.'

'And when did you leave him?'

'Three years ago.'

'Five years together! Did you love him when you married him?'

'I thought I did – more or less. I didn't think much about it. He wanted me.'

'And why did you leave him finally?'

'Because he was unfaithful to me.'

'I believe he still loves you,' said Paul.

'Probably,' she replied.

She was a married woman and believed in simple friend-ship. Paul considered that he was behaving quite correctly towards her. It was only a friendship between man and woman such as any sensible people might have. It seemed to him quite plain. Miriam was his old friend and lover: she belonged to Bestwood and home and his growing up. Clara was a newer friend, and she belonged to Nottingham, to life, to the world. Clara rarely saw Miriam now. They were still friends but the friendship was much weakened.

'Will you come to the concert on Sunday?' Clara asked Paul just after Christmas.

'I promised to go up to Willey Farm,' he replied. 'You're not upset, are you?'

'Why should I be?' she answered.

Again Paul found himself telling her about Miriam.

'She wants me so much that I can't give myself. She wants the **soul** out of my body.'

'And yet you love her?' asked Clara.

'No I don't love her. I never even kiss her.'

'Why not?' Clara asked.

'I don't know.'

'I suppose you're afraid. Anyway, she doesn't want to have your soul. That's your imagination. She wants you.'

He thought about this. Perhaps he was wrong.

'But she seems—' he began.

'You've never tried,' she answered.

CHAPTER ELEVEN

The Test on Miriam

With the spring, the old madness came back to Paul. He did not feel he wanted marriage with Miriam. And yet he wanted to belong to her. It was a powerful need struggling with a still stronger shyness. He had a great tenderness for Miriam. He could not fail her.

Mrs Morel saw him going back to Miriam and was amazed. He said nothing to his mother. He did not explain or excuse himself. If he came home late and she made a comment, he answered coldly:

'I shall come home when I like. I'm old enough.' And his mother went to bed, leaving the door unlocked for him. But she lay awake listening until he came: often long after. It was a great bitterness to her that he had gone back to Miriam.

♦

That summer the **cherry** trees at the farm were heavy with fruit. They stood very tall, hung thick with bright red and dark red drops. Paul and Edgar were gathering the fruit one evening. It had been a hot day and now the clouds were rolling in the sky, dark and warm. The wind made the whole tree swing with a thrilling movement that excited Paul. He sat unsteadily among the higher branches, feeling slightly drunk with the tree's movement, and tore off handful after handful of the smooth, cool fruit. Cherries touched his ears and neck as he leaned forward. Red-coloured fruit glowed under the darkness of the leaves. The sun, going down, caught the broken clouds. Enormous piles of gold shone out in the south-east. The world, until now grey, was bathed by the golden glow, making trees and grass and far-off water shine.

Miriam came out to watch.

'Oh,' Paul heard her call, 'isn't it wonderful!' He looked down. There was a pale light on the soft face turned up to him.

'How high you are!' she said.

He threw a handful of cherries at her. She was taken by surprise and was afraid. He laughed and rained more cherries down on her. She ran off to escape them, picking up some cherries on the way. She hung two fine pairs over her ears, then looked up again.

'Haven't you got enough?' she asked.

'Nearly. It's like being on a ship up here.'

'How long will you stay?'

'Till the sunset ends.'

She watched the gold clouds turn to orange, then rose, then reddish purple, until the passion went out of the sky. Paul climbed down with his basket.

'They're lovely,' said Miriam, feeling the cherries.

He threw a handful of cherries at her. She was taken by surprise and was afraid.

'I've torn my sleeve,' said Paul. It was near the shoulder. She put her fingers through the tear.

'How warm,' she said.

He laughed. There was a strange, new sound in his voice.

'Shall we walk a little way?' he said.

They went down the fields as far as a thick wood.

'Shall we go in among the trees?' he asked.

'Do you want to?'

'Yes.'

It was very dark in the wood. She was afraid. Paul was silent and strange. He seemed hardly conscious of her as a person: to him she was only a woman. He stood against a tree and took her in his arms. She gave herself to him, but as a victim, feeling some sort of horror. This thick-voiced man was a stranger to her.

Later it began to rain. Paul lay with his head on the ground, listening to the sharp sound of the raindrops. His heart was heavy. He realised that she had not been with him, that her soul had stood back. His body felt calmer but that was all. She put her hands over him to feel if he was getting wet.

'We must go,' said Miriam.

'Yes,' said Paul but did not move.

'The rain is coming in on us,' said Miriam.

He rose and helped her up. They walked hand in hand. In a while they went indoors.

They made love a number of times after this. Afterwards Paul always had the feeling of failure and death.

'You don't really want me when I come to you,' said Paul gloomily after a week or two.

'No, don't say so,' she said, taking his head in her arms. 'Don't I want your children?'

'Shall we get married then?' said Paul.

51

'We're too young,' she said, after a pause. 'Not yet.'

With Paul the sense of failure grew stronger. At first it was only a sadness. Then he began to feel he could not go on. He wanted to run, go abroad, anything. Gradually he stopped asking her to have him. He realised consciously that it was no good.

He told his mother that he would break off with Miriam. On Sunday he went up to the farm in the early afternoon. Miriam met him at the end of the farm road. She was wearing a new dress with short sleeves. She had made herself look so beautiful and fresh for him. They sat down. He lay with his head on her breast while she stroked his hair. She knew that he was somehow 'absent'.

'I've been thinking,' he said finally, 'we ought to break it off.'

'What?' she cried in surprise.

'Because it's no good going on. I want us to break off – you to be free of me, I free of you.'

'How many times have you offered to marry me and I wasn't willing?'

'I know – but I want us to break off.'

'You're a child of four!' she said in her anger. 'And what can I tell my mother?' she asked.

'I told my mother that I was breaking it off – cleanly and completely,' he said.

'I shan't tell them at home,' she said. 'It's always been the same: one long battle between us – you fighting me off!'

'Not always – not at first,' he argued.

'Always – from the very beginning – always the same.'

He sat in silence. His heart was hard against her. He left her at the road-end. As she went home alone, in her new dress, having to face her family at the other end, he stood without moving on the high road, filled with pain and shame.

CHAPTER TWELVE

Passion

After leaving Miriam, Paul turned almost immediately to Clara. One evening they went to the cinema and he took her hand in his. She neither moved nor made any sign. On Saturday evening he invited her to have coffee with him after work. Afterwards they walked for a little in the park and in the darkness he caught her suddenly in his arms and kissed her. For the whole of the next day he only thought of seeing her again.

Monday was his half-day at work. He asked her if she would come out with him. They agreed to meet at half-past two. In the bus she leaned against him and he took her hand. They got out beside the river and crossed the bridge. They walked along the path above the river and came to a locked gate. Paul climbed over first. Then Clara climbed up onto it and he held both her hands. Laughing, she looked down into his face. Then she jumped, her breast came against his, he held her and covered her face with kisses.

They decided to go down to the river's edge below. Slipping and sliding, they made their way to the bottom of the steep wooded bank. Paul found a flat place at the foot of two trees. It was covered with wet leaves but it would do. He threw down his raincoat and waved to her to come. She sank down at his side. He pressed his lips to her throat and felt the beat of her blood under his lips. Everything was perfectly still. There was nothing in the afternoon but themselves.

They had a steep climb to get back to the public path at the top. Then they walked into Clifton and had tea at a guest-house. He was madly in love with her now. Every movement she made, every fold in her clothes sent a thrill through him.

Mrs Morel was sitting reading when he got home.

'You're late,' she said, looking at him. His eyes were shining, his face seemed to glow.

'Yes, I've been down at Clifton Grove with Clara. She's – she's awfully nice, Mother. Would you like to know her?'

'Yes,' said Mrs Morel coolly, 'I should like to know what she's like.'

'You don't expect to like her,' said Paul. 'I'll bring her here on Sunday for tea. Shall I bring her?'

'You please yourself,' said Mrs Morel, laughing.

Paul knew that he had won. He mentioned to Miriam that Clara was coming to tea on Sunday.

'I want my mother to meet her,' he added.

'Ah!' There was a silence.

'I may call in before I go to the church service,' Miriam said. 'It's a long time since I saw Clara.'

'Very well,' said Paul, surprised and unconsciously angry.

On the Sunday afternoon, Paul met Clara at Keston station. Clara followed Paul into the house. Mrs Morel rose. The younger woman was very nervous.

'I hope you don't mind my coming,' she said hesitatingly.

'I was pleased when Paul said he would bring you,' replied Mrs Morel. Looking at Paul, she thought what a man he looked in his dark, well-made clothes. Her heart glowed.

She and Clara started talking about Nottingham, Clara still rather nervous, Mrs Morel still rather proud. But they were getting on well together, Paul saw. Mrs Morel measured herself against the younger woman and found herself easily the stronger. Clara was very respectful. She knew how highly Paul thought of his mother and she had been fearful of this meeting, expecting someone hard and cold. She was surprised to find this little, interested woman, chatting so easily with her.

At tea the atmosphere was cool and clear, where everyone was themselves and in tune with the others. Afterwards Paul cleared the table, then walked into the garden, leaving the two women to talk. Clara offered to help wash the dishes and was allowed to dry the tea-things. It was painful for her not to be able to follow him into the garden but at last she allowed herself to go. She went to Paul, who was watching the bees among the autumn flowers.

At that moment Miriam was entering through the garden gate. She saw Clara go up to Paul, saw him turn and saw them move together. Something in the relationship told her that they were already a couple. They were looking into each other's eyes, laughing. At that moment they became conscious of Miriam, and everything changed.

Miriam shook hands with Clara, saying: 'It seems strange to see you here.'

'Yes,' replied the other, 'it seems strange to be here.' There was a pause.

'It is pretty, isn't it?' said Miriam.

'I like it very much,' said Clara.

Then Miriam realised that Clara was accepted here as she could never be. She asked Paul for a book to read. He ran indoors to find one. When he returned, Clara turned to go indoors, leaving him to walk with Miriam to the gate.

'When will you come to Willey Farm?' Miriam called to her.

'I couldn't say,' replied Clara.

'Mother asked me to say she'd be pleased to see you any time.'

'Thank you, but I can't say when.'

'Oh, very well,' said Miriam with some bitterness, and left.

♦

That evening the lovers went out over the fields. Clara leaned against him as they walked, and he held her closer and closer. Suddenly Paul's blood flamed up in him. He caught her in his arms and kissed her again and again. But she was worried about catching her train. They had only fourteen minutes to get to the station, so they ran madly through the darkness. Away to the right they could see the lit-up train approaching. At last Clara fell into the train, completely out of breath. The whistle blew. She was gone.

Before he knew where he was, he found himself back home in the kitchen.

'Do you like her?' he asked his mother, rather unwillingly.

'Yes, I like her. But you'll get tired of her, my son, you know you will. You'd better take some hot milk.'

He refused and went to bed, feeling confused and angry.

CHAPTER THIRTEEN

Baxter Dawes

Paul wanted to see a play which was at the Theatre Royal in Nottingham that week. He asked Clara to come with him. He took his evening clothes in a suitcase and changed at Jordan's after work. At the theatre Clara took off her coat and he discovered she was in a sort of green evening dress that left her arms and neck and part of her breast bare. He could almost feel the firmness and softness of her body as he looked at her. He sat all the evening beside her beautiful bare arm, watching the strong throat, the breasts under the green stuff, the curve of her body in the tight dress. He somehow hated her because she made him suffer the ache of her nearness. When the lights went down, she sank against him and he stroked her hand and arm with his fingers. The play continued but it seemed like a dream, far away from him. The reality was Clara: the white, heavy arms, her throat, her chest rising and falling.

When all was over, the lights up, the people clapping, he came to himself. He helped her on with her coat.

'I love you. You look beautiful in that dress,' he whispered over her shoulder, among the crowd of people. It seemed to him that he met a pair of brown eyes full of hate as they made their way out of the theatre but he did not know whose eyes they were. He and Clara turned away and walked towards the station.

◆

Two or three evenings later, Paul was drinking in the 'Punch Bowl' pub with some of his friends when Baxter Dawes came in. He looked much thinner and seemed to be on a downhill path. His woman, Louie, had left him and he had recently spent a night in jail for fighting. Paul and he were enemies but, as fellow-workers, there was a familiarity between them. Paul often thought about Dawes and wanted to know him better. This evening he offered Dawes a drink. Dawes refused with a curse and went on making insulting references to Paul's friendship with Clara. Paul tried to pay no attention but one final remark caused him to throw half a glass of beer in Dawes's face. There was nearly an ugly fight but the quick-thinking barman led Dawes to the door and forced him to leave the pub.

Paul told Clara jokingly of the quarrel with her husband. The colour rose in her face, her grey eyes glowed with anger. She advised Paul to carry a gun because, she said, Dawes was dangerous. Paul laughed at the idea; but in fact a violent quarrel at the factory a few days later led Dawes

57

to attack Mr Jordan, and ended with Dawes losing his job.

Clara was indeed passionately in love with Paul, and he with her, as far as passion went. One evening they were walking down by the river and his mind was somewhere else. Clara listened to him whistling a sad, dissatisfied tune. She walked on in silence. When they came to a bridge, he sat down, looking at the stars in the water. She sat beside him.

'Will you always stay at Jordan's?' she asked.

'No, I shall leave Nottingham soon and go abroad.'

'Go abroad? What for?'

'I don't know. I feel restless. I shall not go for long, while my mother's there.'

'And if you made a nice lot of money, what would you do?' she asked.

'Live in a pretty house near London with my mother.'

'I see.'

There was a long pause.

'Don't ask me anything about the future,' he said gloomily. 'I don't know anything. Just be with me now.'

She caught him passionately to her, pressing his head down on her breast. She could not mistake the suffering in his voice. And soon the struggle within him died away and he forgot Clara was there any more: only a woman, warm and passionate, there in the dark. And she gave herself to him. She knew how alone he was.

When Paul came to his senses, he realised he was lying on the grass. The warmth he felt was Clara's breathing. What was she? A strong, strange, wild life, breathing with him in the darkness. After such an evening they were both very still, having known the enormous power of passion. But Clara was not satisfied. He might leave her. She had not got him. For Paul, the fire of love slowly died away. He felt more and more that his experience had been impersonal and not with

Clara. He felt a great tenderness for her but it was not she who could keep his soul steady. He had wanted her to be something she could not be.

Once, when they were by themselves, he asked her: 'Do you ever want to marry me?'

'Do *you* want to marry *me*?' she replied.

'Yes, I should like us to have children,' he answered slowly. 'But you don't really want a **divorce** from Baxter, do you?'

It was some minutes before she replied.

'No,' she said, 'I don't think I do.'

Gradually their love-making became more mechanical, without the wonderful high points of that first time.

◆

One night he left her to go to the railway station, over the fields. He did not have much time and it was very dark. He was going through a gate when he saw a dark figure leaning beside it.

'Paul Morel?' said the man.

He knew it was Dawes.

'I've got you, haven't I?' said Dawes.

'I'll miss my train,' said Paul.

'All right then,' answered Dawes, and suddenly the younger man was knocked backwards by a blow across the face. The whole night went black. Then he began to see Dawes more clearly and hit him above the mouth. Suddenly from nowhere came a great blow behind the ear. He heard Dawes's heavy breathing, like a wild animal's. He hung on to the bigger man like a wild cat, till at last Dawes fell with a crash, and Paul went down with him. His hands pressed the other man's throat in a blind need to kill him. Then he was thrown to one side. He felt his enemy kicking him as he lay on his back, helpless, then he lost consciousness.

His hands pressed the other man's throat in a blind need to kill him.

Paul woke gradually. He knew where he was and what had happened but he did not want to move. At last his willpower forced him to get up. He was sick with pain but his brain was clear. He found a pool of water and washed his bloody face and hands. The icy water stung but woke him fully. All he wanted was to get to his mother. On foot, as in a terrible dream, he made the journey home.

Everybody was in bed. His face was raw and badly marked, almost like a dead man's face. The night was a long, bad dream. In the morning he woke to find his mother looking at him. Her blue eyes! They were all he wanted to see. She was there, he was in her hands.

'It's not much, mother,' he said. 'It was Baxter Dawes.' He had a displaced shoulder, and the second day his breathing also became very difficult. His mother was as pale as death and very thin. She sat and looked at him, then looked away into space. Clara came to see him, then Miriam came.

'You know I don't care about them, mother,' he said.

'I'm afraid you don't, my son,' she replied sadly.

People were told it was a bicycle accident and soon he was back at work again.

CHAPTER FOURTEEN

Life at an End

In May Paul decided to spend four days in Blackpool with a friend. His mother went to stay for a week in Sheffield with Annie, who now lived there. Perhaps the change would do her good. Paul arranged to join them on the fifth day and stay in Sheffield till his holiday was over.

His four free days passed enjoyably, without a worry or a

black thought. On the fifth day, Paul ran up the steps of Annie's house, expecting to find his mother laughing in the front room. But it was Annie who opened the door.

'Is Mother ill?' he said.

'Yes, she's not very well. Don't upset her,' Annie replied.

'Is she in bed?'

'Yes.'

A strange feeling came over him. He dropped his bag and ran upstairs. His mother was sitting up in bed. She looked at him almost as if she were ashamed of herself. He saw her greyish colour.

'Mother!' he said.

'I thought you were never coming,' she answered brightly.

But he only fell on his knees at the bedside and buried his face in the blankets, crying in pain. She stroked his hair slowly with her thin hand.

'What is it, Mother?' he said at last.

She said without looking at him: 'It's only a lump, my boy. It's been there for some time.'

His tears rose up again. His mind was hard and clear but his body was crying.

'Where?'

She put her hand on her side to show him. He sat on the bed and took her hand.

'When did you get ill?' he asked.

'It began yesterday,' she answered.

'You ought not to have travelled alone,' he said.

'As if that had anything to do with it,' she answered quickly. 'Now go and have your dinner. They're waiting for you.'

After dinner he went into the kitchen to help Annie wash the dishes. Annie began to cry.

'The pain she had yesterday, I never saw anyone suffer like

it!' she cried. 'Leonard ran like a madman for Dr Ansell. And when she got to bed, she said to me, "Annie, look at this lump on my side. I wonder what it is." And when I looked, I nearly dropped. It's a lump as big as an apple. I said, "Good heavens, mother, whenever did that come?" "Why, child," she said, "it's been there a long time." She's been having these pains for months at home and nobody looking after her.'

'But she's been seeing the doctor in Nottingham, she says, and she never told me,' he said.

In the afternoon he went to see Dr Ansell, a wise, lovable man.

'Can't you operate?' asked Paul.

'Not there,' said the doctor.

'Might it be **cancer**?'

'I don't know. I would like an examination by her regular doctor, Dr Jameson, but you must arrange it. He will charge you not less than ten pounds to come all the way from Nottingham.'

Paul agreed to make the arrangement and went to see Dr Jameson in Nottingham two days later. He was friendly, busy, kind. He agreed to come to Sheffield the next day, a Sunday. Paul went home to see his father. They now employed a little serving girl called Minnie, and she was looking after him. Paul had written him a letter to tell him about his wife but his father was afraid to mention her. They ate in silence.

'Well, and how is she?' asked the old miner at last.

'She can sit up – we can carry her down for tea,' said Paul. 'You must go and see her next week, father.'

'I hope she'll be home by that time,' said Morel.

'If she's not,' said Paul, 'you must come.'

Dr Jameson came on the Sunday, as agreed, together with Dr Ansell. The examination did not take long. Arthur, Paul and Leonard waited nervously for the two doctors to come downstairs. They were told that an operation was impossible: Mrs Morel's heart was too weak; but it might be possible to reduce the lump by using suitable drugs.

Paul had to go back to work. On the Saturday Walter Morel took the train to Sheffield. When he arrived, he looked lost. The old man came into the bedroom rather fearfully.

'How do I find you, my girl?' he said, kissing her hurriedly and shyly.

'Well, I'm half and half,' she replied.

'I can see you are,' he said, looking down on her. Then he wiped his eyes with his handkerchief and sat looking at her almost as if she was a stranger.

Mrs Morel did not change much. She stayed in Sheffield for two months. At the end of that time she was, if anything, rather worse, but she wanted to go home. So they got a motorcar from Nottingham because she was too ill to go by train. Morel knew she was coming: he had the front door open. Half the neighbours came out to greet her. Mrs Morel, smiling, drove home down the street. They saw her smile and nod. It was a great event in Bestwood.

Morel wanted to carry her inside but he was too old. Arthur picked her up as if she was a child. They put a big, deep chair near the fire, where her old chair used to stand. When she was unwrapped and sitting down and had drunk a little wine, she looked round the room.

'Don't think I didn't like your house, Annie,' she said, 'but it's good to be in my own home again.'

And Morel added in a shaky voice:

'It is, girl, it is.'

While Paul was in Sheffield, he heard from Dr Ansell that a man from Nottingham was in the local fever hospital. He was none other than Baxter Dawes. Paul decided to visit him.

It appeared that Dawes had come to take up work in Sheffield but after only a day or two had fallen seriously ill. Paul told him about his mother's illness and offered to visit him again when he returned to Sheffield. Back in Nottingham, he told Clara about Dawes. She seemed very upset by the news.

'Is he very bad?' she asked guiltily.

'He has been. He's improving now.'

There was a distance now between the lovers.

'I've behaved badly to him,' she said, 'and now you're behaving badly to me. It's what I deserve. He loved me a thousand times better than you ever did.'

As soon as she could, she went to Sheffield to see her husband. The meeting was not a success; but she left him roses and fruit and money. She wanted to repay him, even though her heart was not warm with love.

Mrs Morel got gradually worse. Paul knew, and she knew, that she was dying but they kept up a pretence of cheerfulness.

Dawes was now in a rest home near Nottingham and Paul visited him there sometimes. A peculiar friendship developed between the two men. Dawes, still very weak, seemed to rely on Paul.

The days and weeks went by. December came, and some snow. Paul stayed at home all the time now. They could not afford a nurse, so Paul shared the nursing with Annie. Their mother had strong drugs every night to help her sleep and her heart beat irregularly. Annie slept beside her. Paul went in in the early morning when his sister got up. Mrs Morel's eyes grew darker and darker, her body thinner, her skin greyer.

'Can't you give her something to put an end to it?' he asked the doctor at last.

But the doctor shook his head.

Walter Morel was silent and frightened. Sometimes he

went into the sickroom to look at her, then left in confusion.

One evening Paul collected all the sleeping pills there were and took them downstairs. Carefully he made them into a powder. He put the powder into the hot milk which he took to his mother at nine o'clock. She drank a little and looked at him with dark, wondering eyes.

'Oh, it *is* bitter, Paul,' she said, making an expression of distaste.

'It's to help you sleep better,' he said.

She drank some more of the milk. 'Oh, it *is* horrible,' she told him.

Paul brought her a little cold milk to take away the taste. Mrs Morel drank it down. She was sighing with tiredness. Her heartbeat was very irregular. Paul and Annie settled her down for the night. As usual, Annie slept with her and Paul slept in the next room. He was woken suddenly by Annie's whispered: 'Paul – Paul! Come and look at her!'

His mother lay with her cheek on her hand, in the same position as before. But her mouth had fallen open and she was breathing with loud, heavy breaths, with long pauses in between. They sat silently listening to the great rough breaths. The night went by breath by breath. Still it was dark. His father got up.

'Had I better stay?' he whispered.

'No – go to work,' answered Paul. In a few minutes he heard his father's heavy footsteps on the snow outside. He watched the snow growing blue. A grey, deathly dawn followed. Annie came in and looked at him questioningly.

'Just the same,' he said calmly.

Soon the neighbours came with their frightened question: 'How is she?'

At ten o'clock the district nurse came.

'Nurse!' cried Paul, 'she'll continue like this for days.'

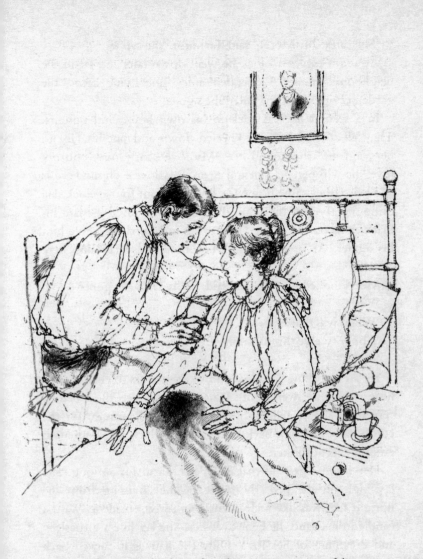

'Oh, it is bitter, Paul,' she said, *making an expression of distaste*.

'She can't, Mr Morel,' said the nurse, 'she can't.'

At about eleven o'clock he went downstairs and sat in the neighbours' house. Suddenly Annie came flying across the garden crying: 'Paul – Paul – She's gone!'

In a second he was back in his own house and upstairs. They all stood back. He kneeled down and put his face to hers and his arms round her: 'My love – my love – oh my love,' he whispered again and again. 'My love – oh my love.'

Their father came home from work about four o'clock. He came silently into the house and sat down. Tired, he laid his black arms on the table. The serving girl hurried to give him his dinner. At last Paul said: 'You noticed the curtains were closed?'

Morel looked up. 'No!' he said, 'Why? Has she gone?'

'Yes.'

'When was that?'

'About twelve this morning.'

'Hm.'

He ate his dinner, washed and went upstairs to change. In a little while he went out. Paul went to get the doctor's certificate and to tell the men to come and measure for the coffin. When he got back about eight o'clock, the house was empty, except for her.

Her room was cold that had been warm for so long. She lay high on the bed, the shape of the covering from the upright feet was like a clean curve of snow, so silent. With a candle in his hand, he bent over her. She lay like a girl asleep and dreaming of her love. Only the hair as it curved back from her face was mixed with silver.

After two days the relations came for the funeral and the children had to welcome them. They buried her next to William in a terrible storm of rain and wind. The wet earth and all the white flowers shone with rain. Annie held Paul's arm and leaned forward. Down below, she saw a dark corner of William's coffin. The wooden box sank steadily. She was gone. The rain poured down and the crowd in black with their umbrellas turned away. The burial ground was empty under the pouring rain.

Paul went home and kept himself busy passing round drinks to the guests. His father sat in the kitchen with Mrs Morel's relations and cried, saying what a good woman she'd been and how he'd tried to do everything he could for her. Paul hated his father for his self-pity.

CHAPTER FIFTEEN

The Death of Hope

Paul felt lonely and defeated. His mother had really supported his life. He wanted someone to help him, of their own choosing. But Clara was not strong enough for him to hold on to. She wanted him, but did not want to understand him. If no one was willing to help him, he would go on alone.

Baxter Dawes was almost completely recovered from his illness. He had found a job and a place to live in Sheffield. He was going to start work on Monday. Paul knew that his own relationship with Clara was over and that she would go back to Dawes. She did in fact go with her husband to Sheffield and Paul scarcely saw her again.

There was little affectionate feeling between father and son. As there was no one to keep the home together, and as neither of them could accept the emptiness of the house, Paul took a room in Nottingham and Morel went to live with a friendly family in Bestwood.

Paul's life had fallen to pieces. He could not paint. At work there was no Clara. There was nothing left. Everything seemed so different, so unreal. There seemed no reason why people should walk along the street or why houses should stand in their places. The most real thing to him was the thick darkness of night. That seemed whole and meaningful and restful. Sitting alone in his room, he heard two voices in his head.

'What am I doing?'

'Destroying myself.'

'That's wrong.'

'Why wrong?'

'She's dead. What was it all for, her struggle?'

'You're alive. You've got to stay alive for her sake, carry on for her. Go on with your painting.'

'Painting is not living.'

'Marry then, have children.'

'Marry who?'

'Miriam.'

But he did not trust this answer. Always alone, his soul swung first to the side of death, then stubbornly to the side of life. The real disaster was that he had nowhere to go, nothing to do, nothing to say and *was* nothing himself. He felt completely disconnected from other people.

He went by chance to church one Sunday evening, and there was Miriam a few rows in front of him. He found her outside after the service.

'What are you doing in town?' he asked.

'I'm staying at my cousin Anne's – just till tomorrow.'

He invited her to come back to his room for supper. They took the bus and scarcely spoke until they reached his place, on the edge of town. In his room supper was laid. Paul made coffee. Miriam told him shyly that she was going to train as a teacher at Broughton College.

'I suppose you're glad,' said Paul.

'Very glad.'

'Well, you'll find earning your own living isn't everything.'

After supper they sat by the fire facing each other.

'You've broken off with Clara?' Miriam asked.

'Yes.'

'You know,' she said, 'I think we ought to be married.'

'Why?'

'You're wasting yourself like this.'

'I'm not sure,' he said slowly, 'that marriage would be much good. You want to put me in your pocket and I would die there.'

'What will you do instead?' she asked.

'I don't know – go on, I suppose. Perhaps I'll go abroad.'

There was a long silence.

'Will you have me, to marry me?' he said in a very low voice.

'Do you want it?' she asked, deeply serious.

'Not much,' he replied with pain. 'And without marriage we can do nothing?'

'No,' she said, her voice like a deep bell. 'No, I think not.'

He went with her to her cousin's house and left her there. As he turned away, he felt the last foothold for him had gone. The town stretched away to the distance, a flat sea of lights. Behind him lay the country, with little points of light for more towns – the sea – the night – on and on! On every side the enormous dark silence seemed to be pressing him into nothingness; and yet, though so small and unimportant, he was *not* nothing.

'Mother!' he whispered in sharpest pain, 'Mother!' She was the only thing that helped him to remain himself among all this. And she was gone, a part of the earth again.

But no, he would not give in. He straightened himself and closed his lips firmly. He would not take that direction, to the darkness, to follow her. He walked towards the distant noise, the glowing golden lights of the city, quickly.

EXERCISES

Vocabulary Work

Look back at the 'Dictionary Words' in this book. Check that you know their meanings.

1 Find words which mean the same as these phrases:
   a a public show of objects or pictures
   b a box used to bury a dead person
   c a place where minerals are taken out of the ground
   a a simple kind of light, made of wax
   e a small red fruit
   f an instrument or machine
   g an agreement to get married
   h the way to cook bread, cakes etc.

2 Write sentences combining these words to show their meaning clearly.
   a passion/soul   c sensitive/divorce
   b to swing/elastic   d cancer/to faint

Comprehension

Chapters 1–3
   1 What did Walter Morel do to his wife when they had their first big quarrel?
   2 What did Morel hide behind the coalhouse door? Why?

Chapters 4–6
   3 Where did Paul get a job after he left school?
   4 What did William say about Lily Western that proved to be correct after his death?

73

Discussion

1 In this story Walter Morel always appears in an unfavourable light (eg insensitive, uneducated, cruel, a heavy drinker etc). Consider how family life might be seen through his eyes and how some of his behaviour might be better understood, if not always excused.

2 Is Paul more successful as a son than as a lover? Why do you think so?

Writing

1 Imagine that you are William, living in London. Write a letter to your mother, Mrs Morel, telling her about your work, your pleasures and your girlfriend. Your letter can be about a page long.

2 Imagine a meeting between Miriam and Clara just after the end of the story, during which they discuss and compare their opinions of Paul: his good and bad points. Write the conversation between the two women. Write about a page.

Review

Write a note to one of your friends, telling him or her about this book. like or dislike it.